TO:Remi

love:Cousin Erick

I hope you enjoy
your book!

Love,
Tia Ang
&
Tio ERICK

g A GOLDEN BOOK • NEW YORK

KOHL'S
Style 97609
Factory Number 126509
Production Date 01/2017

Ages 3 and up

MANUFACTURED IN CHINA
10 9 8 7 6 5 4 3 2 1

The POKY LITTLE PUPPY

by JANETTE SEBRING LOWREY

illustrated by GUSTAF TENGGREN

FIVE little puppies dug a hole under the fence
and went for a walk in the wide, wide world.
Through the meadow they went, down the
road, over the bridge, across the green grass,
and up the hill, one right after the other.

And when they got to the top of the hill,
they counted themselves: *one, two, three, four.*
One little puppy wasn't there.

"Now where in the world is that poky little
puppy?" they wondered. For he certainly
wasn't on top of the hill.

He wasn't going down the other side. The only thing they could see going down was a fuzzy caterpillar.

He wasn't coming up this side. The only
thing they could see coming up was a quick
green lizard.

But when they looked down at the grassy place
near the bottom of the hill, there he was, running
round and round, his nose to the ground.

"What is he doing?" the four little puppies asked one another. And down they went to see, roly-poly, pell-mell, tumble-bumble, till they came to the green grass; and there they stopped short.

"What in the world are you doing?" they asked.

"I smell something!" said the poky little puppy.

Then the four little puppies began to sniff, and they smelled it, too.

"Rice pudding!" they said.

And home they went, as fast as they could go, over the bridge, up the road, through the meadow, and under the fence. And there, sure enough, was dinner waiting for them, with rice pudding for dessert.

But their mother was greatly displeased. "So you're the little puppies who dig holes under fences!" she said. "No rice pudding tonight!" And she made them go straight to bed.

But the poky little puppy came home after everyone was sound asleep.

He ate up the rice pudding and crawled into bed as happy as a lark.

The next morning someone had filled the hole and put up a sign. The sign said:

BUT . . . . .
The five little puppies dug a hole under the fence, just the same, and went for a walk in the wide, wide world.

Through the meadow they went, down the road, over the bridge, across the green grass, and up the hill, two and two. And when they got to the top of the hill, they counted themselves: *one, two, three, four.* One little puppy wasn't there.

"Now where in the world is that poky little puppy?" they wondered. For he certainly wasn't on top of the hill.

He wasn't going down the other side. The only thing they could see going down was a big black spider.

He wasn't coming up this side. The
only thing they could see coming up was
a brown hop-toad.

But when they looked down at the grassy
place near the bottom of the hill, there was
the poky little puppy, sitting still as a stone, with
his head on one side and his ears cocked up.

"What is he doing?" the four little puppies asked
one another. And down they went to see, roly-
poly, pell-mell, tumble-bumble, till they came to
the green grass; and there they stopped short.

"What in the world are you doing?" they asked.

"I hear something!" said the poky little puppy.

The four little puppies listened, and they
could hear it, too. "Chocolate custard!" they cried.
"Someone is spooning it into our bowls!"

And home they went as fast as they could
go, over the bridge, up the road, through the
meadow, and under the fence. And there,
sure enough, was dinner waiting for them,
with chocolate custard for dessert.

But their mother was greatly displeased. "So you're the little puppies who *will* dig holes under fences!" she said. "No chocolate custard tonight!" And she made them go straight to bed.

But the poky little puppy came home after everyone else was sound asleep, and he

ate up all the chocolate custard and crawled into bed as happy as a lark.

The next morning someone had filled the hole and put up a sign.

The sign said:

BUT. . .

In spite of that, the five little puppies dug a hole under the fence and went for a walk in the wide, wide world.

Through the meadow they went, down the road, over the bridge, across the green grass, and up the hill, two and two. And when they got to the top of the hill, they counted themselves: *one, two, three, four.* One little puppy wasn't there.

"Now where in the world is that poky little puppy?" they wondered. For he certainly wasn't on top of the hill.

He wasn't going down the other side.
The only thing they could see going
down was a little grass snake.

He wasn't coming up this side. The only
thing they could see coming up was a big
grasshopper.

But when they looked down at the grassy place near the bottom of the hill, there he was, looking hard at something on the ground in front of him.

"What is he doing?" the four little puppies asked one another. And down they went to see, roly-poly, pell-mell, tumble-bumble, till they came to the green grass; and there they stopped short.

"What in the world are you doing?" they asked.

"I see something!" said the poky little puppy.
The four little puppies looked, and they
could see it, too. It was a ripe, red strawberry
growing there in the grass.

"Strawberry shortcake!" they cried.

And home they went as fast as they could go, over the bridge, up the road, through the meadow, and under the fence. And there, sure enough, was dinner waiting for them, with strawberry shortcake for dessert.

But their mother said: "So you're the little puppies who dug that hole under the fence again! No strawberry shortcake for supper tonight!" And she made them go straight to bed.

But the four little puppies waited till they thought she was asleep, and then they slipped out and filled up the hole, and when they turned around, there was their mother watching them.

"What good little puppies!" she said. "Come have some strawberry shortcake!"

And this time, when the poky little puppy got home, he had to squeeze in through a wide place in the fence. And there were his four brothers and sisters, licking the last crumbs from their saucer.

"Dear me!" said his mother. "What a pity you're so poky! Now the strawberry shortcake is all gone!"

So the poky little puppy had to go to bed without a single bite of shortcake, and he felt very sorry for himself.

And the next morning someone had put
up a sign that read:

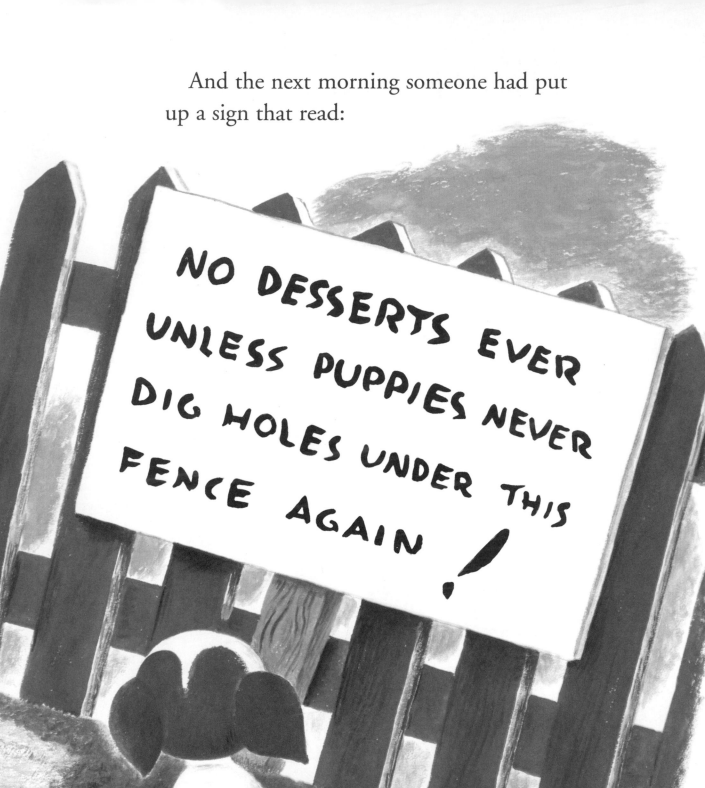

NO DESSERTS EVER
UNLESS PUPPIES NEVER
DIG HOLES UNDER THIS
FENCE AGAIN!

Animal Orchestra

by ILO ORLEANS

illustrated by TIBOR GERGELY

In Animal Town
It was Musical Day.
The orchestra
Had gathered to play.

Everyone came
To hear and to see.

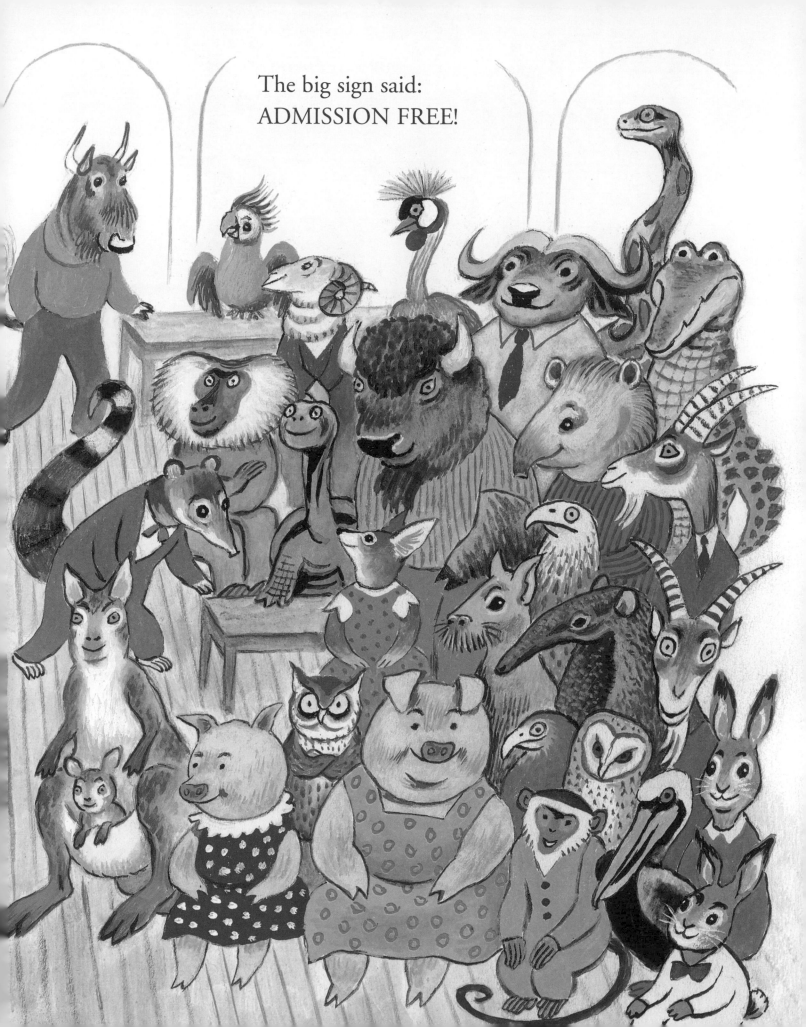

The big sign said:
ADMISSION FREE!

Up to the platform
Each animal went,

And proudly carried
His instrument.

Then came the conductor
With stick in his hand—
The handsomest Hippo
In Animal Land.
He tapped his foot.
He waved his hand,
And cried to the players:
"Strike up the band!"

The gray Seals barked.
They lifted their fins,
And tweedled upon
Their violins.

The spotted Giraffes—
The oddest fellows—
Zoomed and zoomed
On their yellow cellos.

The Lion bugled;
The Rhino fluted;

The Leopard harped;
The Tiger tooted.

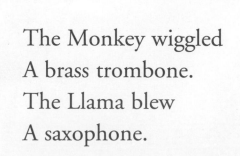

The Monkey wiggled
A brass trombone.
The Llama blew
A saxophone.

The Elephant
Kept trumpeting.
The Camel plucked
His mandolin string.

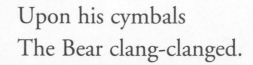

Upon his cymbals
The Bear clang-clanged.

Upon his guitar
The Fox twang-twanged!

The Yak beat the drum;
The Wolf played the fife.
Each beast was enjoying
The time of his life.

They whistled! They fiddled!
They thumped! They blew!

What a roar! What a din!
What a great to-do!

The animal girls—
The animal boys—
The animal audience
Made a great noise.

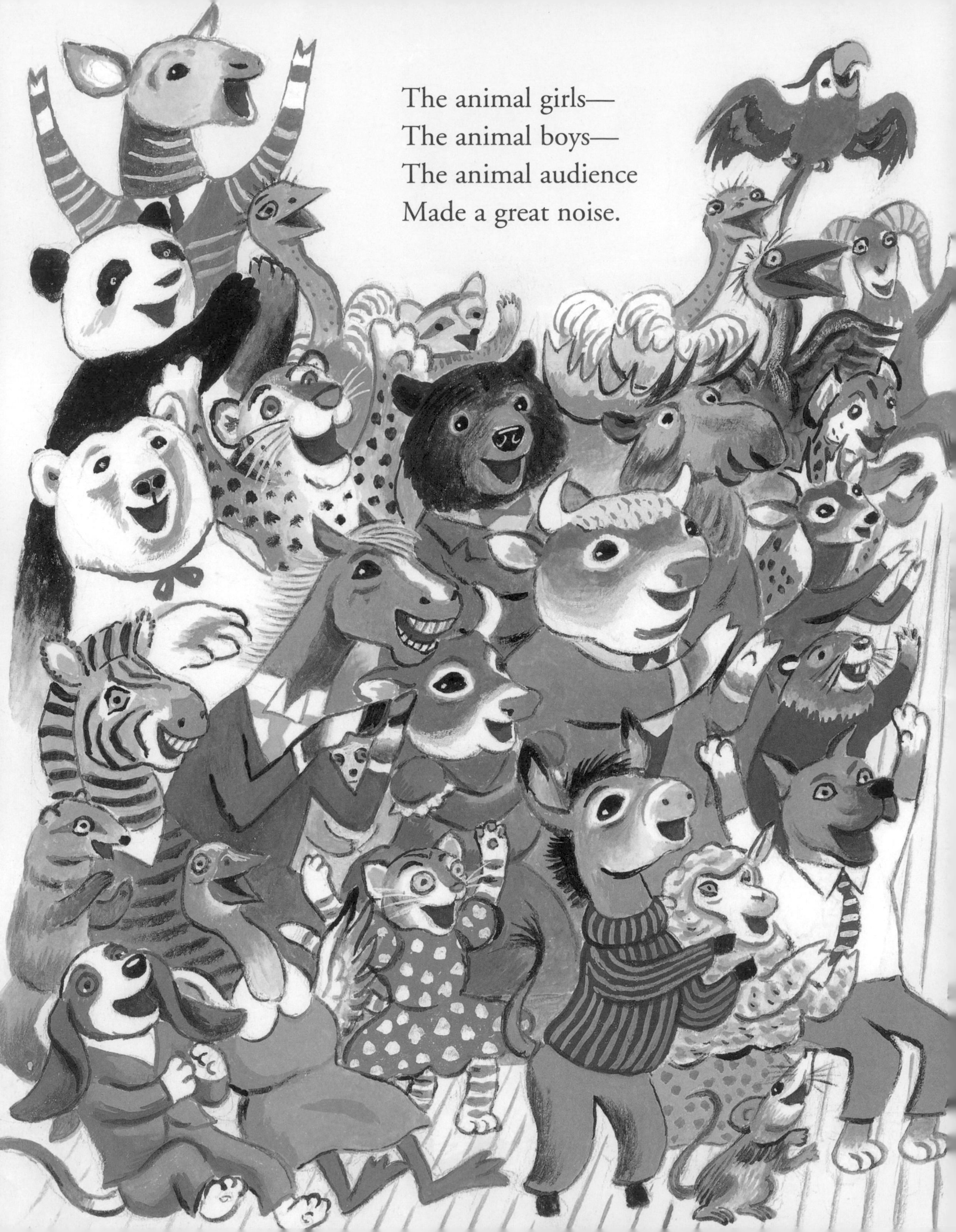

They slapped their tails,
They clapped their paws,
And that is how
They made applause!

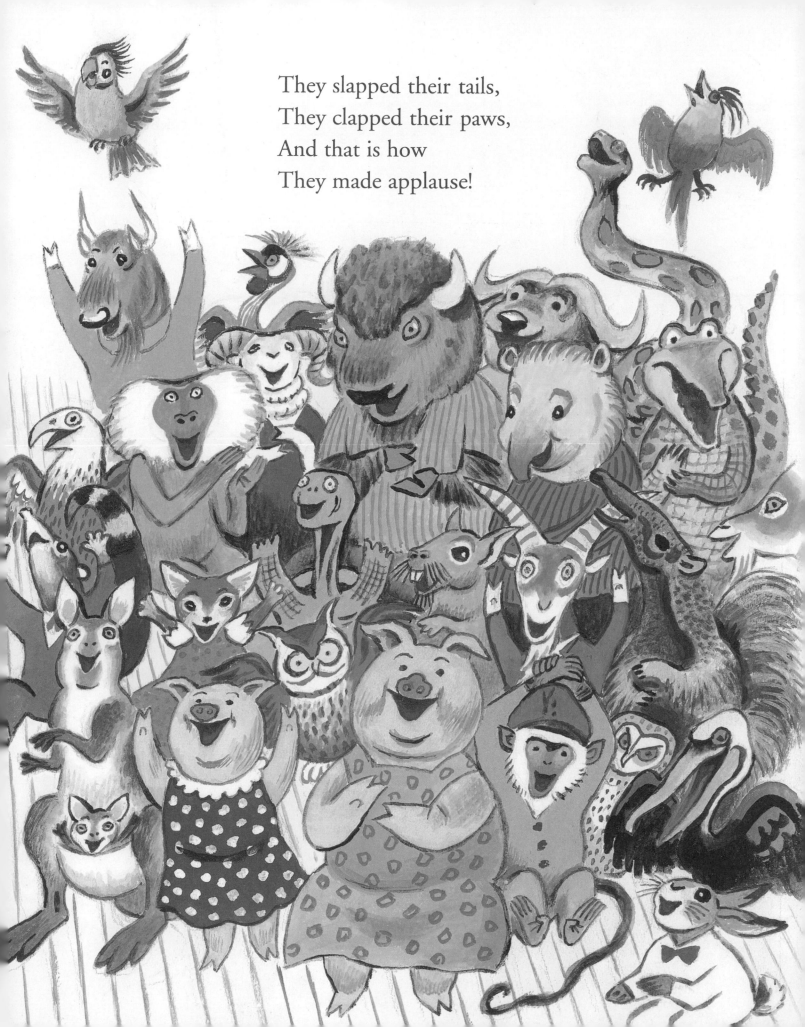

The conductor bowed,
And bowed and bowed.

All of the orchestra
Players were proud.

The Hippo was happy
On Musical Day,
For everyone shouted:
"Hip-HIPPO-ray!"

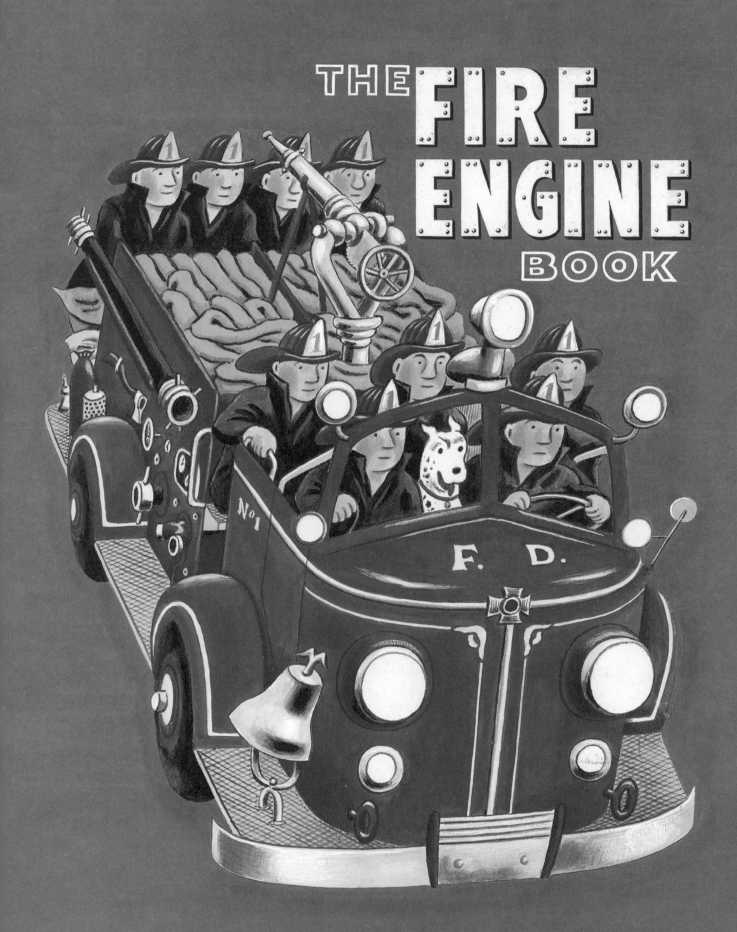

THE FIRE ENGINE BOOK

illustrated by TIBOR GERGELY

Ding, ding, ding! goes the alarm.

The firemen slide down the pole.

Clang, clang, clang! goes the fire engine bell.

The chief is on his way.

Here they come!

Watch out! Make way for the hose car.

Hurry, hurry! Jump on the hook-and-ladder truck!

The people come running out to see

the great big hook-and-ladder truck.

Here they are at the fire.

The chief tells his men what to do.

Quick! Connect the hoses!

S-s-s-s! goes the water.

Crank, crank. Up go the ladders.

Up go the firemen with their hoses.

Chop, chop, chop! go the axes.

Crash! go the windows.

Down the ladders come the firemen.

They jump into the net to save things from the fire!

Sput, sput, sput! Out goes the fire.

Tired firemen and people go home.

Hurray for the brave firemen!